A catalogue record for this book is available
from the British Library

Published by Ladybird Books Ltd
A subsidiary of the Penguin Group
A Pearson Company

LADYBIRD and the device of a Ladybird are trademarks of
Ladybird Books Ltd Loughborough Leicestershire UK

© Disney MCMXCVIII

Adapted from Walt Disney Pictures' **Mulan**

Music by Matthew Wilder   Lyrics by David Zippel   Original score by Jerry Goldsmith
Produced by Pam Coats
Directed by Barry Cook and Tony Bancroft

Long ago, in a village in Ancient China, there was a young woman, named Mulan. She lived with her father, Fa Zhou, her mother, Fa Li, and her grandmother.

Fa Zhou had once been a famous soldier. But the country had been at peace for many years, and he did not expect to have to fight again.

Today was an important day for Mulan.
She was going to meet the Matchmaker.
But Mulan was very late getting ready.

Fa Li quickly added the family comb as
the final touch. Then Mulan hurried away
to join the line outside the Matchmaker's
house. She was the first to be called in.

The Matchmaker asked Mulan to pour some tea. "You must demonstrate dignity and refinement," the Matchmaker told her.

But this wasn't easy – especially when Cri-Kee, Mulan's lucky cricket, decided to help. Soon tea spilled over the table, an incense-burner fell to the floor, and the Matchmaker's dress caught fire… It was a disaster, and Mulan got the blame.

The Matchmaker was furious. "You may look like a bride," she screamed at Mulan, "but you will never bring your family honour!"

Mulan's mother and grandmother led her away. The whole Fa Family was in disgrace.

Mulan removed her comb and sat sadly in the garden. She thought about what had happened. *What would her father say? Was the Matchmaker right? Would she never bring honour to her family?*

"What beautiful blossoms!" said a quiet voice beside her.

It was her father, pointing at a bud in the tree. "Look, this one is late. When it blooms, it will be the most beautiful of all." He put Mulan's comb back in her hair.

Mulan smiled. She was forgiven.

Suddenly, drums rolled in the distance and a crowd gathered in the village. There was very bad news. The enemy, Shan-Yu and the Huns, had invaded China. *By order of the Emperor, one man from every family must serve in the Imperial Army.*

Fa Zhou was called to fight again, for the honour of his family and his country.

That night, as rain beat heavily on the Temple statue, Mulan was lost in thought. She was worried about her father. *Why should he have to go to war? He's too old and lame to fight now. But how can I stop him?*

Suddenly Mulan had an idea…

As lightning flashed around her, she stole into her parent's room, picked up Fa Zhou's army papers and replaced them with her comb. Then, dressed in her father's armour and sword, she took her father's horse and rode off into the night.

A crash of thunder woke the family. They found Mulan was gone! She had taken Fa Zhou's place in the Army.

Throughout the night, wind gusted through the Fa Family Temple. Shadows danced across the walls.

"Mushu… awaken!" came the voice of the First Ancestor, and an incense-burner transformed at once into a tiny dragon.

The Ancestors ordered Mushu to go outside and wake the Great Stone Dragon – this was the Fa Family Guardian, chosen by the Ancestors to protect Mulan.

Reluctantly, Mushu climbed the Great Stone Dragon and banged its head with his gong.

CRRRUUNNCH! The statue crumbled beneath him. *Oh, no! Who would help Mulan now?*

Cri-Kee chirped and suggested Mushu should go instead.

"That's it!" cried Mushu, triumphantly. "I'll do it. I'll make Mulan a hero, and then *I'll* be made a proper Guardian." So, joining forces with Cri-Kee, Mushu went to find Mulan.

Mulan was on a cliff, overlooking the Imperial Army Training Camp. "Who am I fooling?" she said to her horse, Khan. "It's going to take a miracle to get me into the Army."

"Did I hear someone ask for a miracle?" said a powerful voice behind her. Mushu grandly introduced himself as her Ancestral Guardian.

Mulan turned to see a tiny creature with Cri-Kee. "My Ancestors have sent a little lizard to help me?" she asked, puzzled.

"Dragon!" corrected Mushu. "Not lizard. And, of course, I'm travel-size for your convenience."

Mulan still wasn't sure, but knowing she would need all the help she could get, she decided to follow Mushu's advice and went to join the Army.

Mulan's first day went very badly. She accidentally started a fight with three of the new recruits and within minutes the whole Camp was in chaos.

Shang, the Imperial Army Captain, swiftly brought the troops to order. He spoke sternly to Mulan, "I don't need anyone causing trouble in the Camp. Show me your army papers!"

Mulan nervously handed them over. Shang was surprised to learn that the Great Fa Zhou had a son. But he accepted it. Her secret was safe for the moment.

Captain Shang ordered the recruits to tidy up. "Your training starts tomorrow. And you all have a lot to learn."

Later, when the training was complete, Captain Shang led the way over the long mountain pass. All around were signs of a fierce battle, and black smoke curled up into the sky. The Main Army had been destroyed.

Suddenly
Shan-Yu and his
soldiers surrounded them.
Flaming arrows showered
down on Shang's men.

"Prepare to fight," cried Shang.
"If we die, we die with honour."

But Mulan had a different idea. She
fired the cannon into the mountains and
triggered off an avalanche. Shan-Yu struck
her with his sword, but she saw Shang
buried in the snow and went to rescue him.

Soon the enemy was engulfed in snow.
Shang and his soldiers proclaimed Mulan
the Hero, but she collapsed in pain.

Mulan awoke in the doctor's tent, surrounded by angry faces. She knew at once that her secret had been discovered.

She was a disgrace to the Imperial Army. It was Captain Shang's duty to kill her.

Shang held a sword above Mulan's head. "A life for a life," he said firmly. "My debt is repaid." Then he threw the sword down, and ordered the troops to go home.

Mulan was left in the mountains.

Meanwhile Shan-Yu's falcon flew high above the mountain pass. It screeched and dived down, as its master's arm thrust up through the snow.

Then Mulan and her friends watched in horror as Shan-Yu and five of his warriors climbed out of their snowy graves. "Perfect!" said Shan-Yu. "Now for the Imperial City!"

Mulan didn't hesitate. She picked up her sword and raced away on Khan. Mushu and Cri-Kee followed swiftly behind.

In the Imperial City, everyone gathered to celebrate the Army's victory.

Mulan struggled to find a way through the crowds. She spotted Shang and tried to warn him that the Emperor was in danger. But the Captain turned away, refusing to trust her a second time.

As the Emperor came forward to honour the troops, Shan-Yu came out of hiding and his men emerged from their paper dragon.

Taking everyone by surprise, they captured the Emperor and held him prisoner in a palace tower.

Shang and his soldiers couldn't get in. But Mulan beckoned them to follow her. They trusted her now. She disguised herself and three soldiers, Ling, Yao, and Chien-Po, as palace maidens, and led the way to the tower entrance.

They diverted the Huns' attention, while Shang ran upstairs. Then they overpowered the Hun guards and raced to the rescue.

As Shang fought with
Shan-Yu, Mulan and her friends
helped the Emperor to get away to safety.

Shan-Yu was furious and prepared to
kill Shang. "You took away my victory!"
he roared.

"No, I did!" said Mulan, and she pulled
back her hair.

Shan-Yu recognised her at once, "The
soldier from the mountains!"

Then, furious, he chased Mulan out onto the roof. "It looks like you're out of ideas," he sneered.

"Not quite," answered Mulan. "Ready, Mushu?" A burning rocket flew towards them and hit Shan-Yu. It sent him crashing into the munitions tower.

Mulan slid down to the ground, where she landed on Shang. She hugged him, pleased to see he had escaped unharmed. They watched together, as fireworks exploded around them and a fireball engulfed the palace.

Now Mulan had to face the Emperor. "I've heard a good deal about you, Fa Mulan," he said sternly. "You stole your father's armour, ran away from home, impersonated a soldier, dishonoured the Chinese Army, destroyed my palace and… you saved us all."

Then bowing to Mulan, the Emperor presented his medallion and Shan-Yu's sword. "These will show your family what you have done for me and for China."

The next day, Mulan gave her father the Emperor's gifts. "These are to honour the Fa Family," she said. Fa Zhou gave her a big hug. "The greatest honour is having you for a daughter."

As Shang came into the garden and was welcomed by the family, Mushu and the Ancestors watched them from the Temple. Mushu nudged the First Ancestor and said, "Okay! Who did a good job, then?" And Mushu was made a Guardian at last.